The Time Golem

A Novelette

Seth Schindler

ELJ Editions, Ltd. is committed to publishing works of quality and integrity. In that spirit, we are proud to offer this novelette collection to our readers. This novelette is a work of fiction. Names, characters, places, and incidents either are the product of the author's imagination or are used fictitiously, and any resemblance to actual persons, living or dead, business establishments, events, or locales is entirely coincidental.

ISBN: 978-1-941617-76-2

Cover Design by Susan E. French

ELJ Publications (Imprint)
ELJ Editions, Ltd.
P.O. Box 815
Washingtonville, NY 10992

www.elj-editions.com

To my family
To all those who survived
And mostly to the millions who didn't
Never again

It was larger than life. As it should be. As they all were. Except for the very first. Adam.

David stepped back and craned his head to see the top of the sculpture. He wished he could've been more faithful to the original in the Garden and the ones constructed by medieval kabbalists in Prague. Whether formed of desert dust, beach sand or river mud, what mattered only was that a golem emerged from the earth itself.

Crafted of steel-reinforced plaster, his version was far from ideal. David had loved making it anyway. Still, he knew he probably should've made it smaller, certainly much lighter; it almost touched the studio's ten-foot ceiling and weighed half a ton. He'd need a forklift to put the colossus in the pickup truck. And it'd be a bitch to get it in the gallery for the one-man show.

David pictured the sculpture stuck in the gallery's stylish doorway and laughed. Lately, he didn't think that far ahead. Neither did golems, legend had it. Just Do It could've been their motto. Today was all that mattered to them. And now to him. When he knew his next breath might just be his last. Or that it wasn't really him who was breathing. Maybe the Zen master Alan's message to him all those years ago had finally sunk in.

He moved closer to the portable swamp cooler. Not

that it would make a difference. The thing barely made a dent in the oppressive humid heat of August. This morning, he could have sworn he smelled rain when he walked his dog Lacy through the creosote and prickly pears behind his house. The monsoon season came later and the rains less often than when he'd lived in Tucson the first time. Now, the clouds hung back, only teasing a respite.

David removed his sweat-stained T-shirt and fanned himself with a piece of cardboard. He scratched the long scar on his chest that still itched. Not that he ever minded scratching it—feeling his heart still beating.

He'd just applied the matte sealer after putting the final touches to the painted patina of the sculpture's lower two sections: muted earth colors, mostly browns and greens for the eight-foot-long, four-foot-wide quasi-human male figure lying on its back on the floor and the six-foot-tall gnarled tree trunk growing vertically out of its belly. The surface of the three-foot-high pyramidical shrine, mounted atop the tree trunk, glittered with a metallic gold bas-relief composed of etched numbers and a riot of red, blue, and black highly stylized Hebrew letters, some of which seemingly formed words. Resting inside the shrine was his favorite part, a vintage factory punch clock.

The phlegmy crackle of a smoker's cough broke the silence, and the musty scent of a stale fifty-cent cigar hit David's nose. He smiled and turned to find Charlie's large frame—all six foot five, two hundred eighty pounds of him—filling the doorway. He wore his usual tattered overalls, a ratty sombrero on his head, a bottle in one hand, a fat Dutch Masters President in his mouth. Charlie had the adjoining studio, identical to his, a dilapidated, windowless Army-surplus Quonset hut next to the railroad tracks in a shabby industrial area. He did ornamental welded metalwork. Custom gates and fences were his bread and butter, though he preferred making whimsical sculptures of desert animals and plants, what they called "yard art" in Tucson.

"What the fuck's that?" Charlie pointed his cigar at the sculpture as he approached David in the back of the studio.

David stepped toward Charlie and hugged him. "I've missed you, you ugly bastard."

Charlie punched David's shoulder. "And you're as crazy as ever."

"*You* should talk! Still smoking—"

"Why not? I'll probably be dead anyway come next summer. And I'm celebrating today, so give me a fucking break. Just finished my last Big C treatment." He passed David the bottle. "Go ahead, open it. My hands are still shaky."

David glanced at the bottle. "Champagne?"

Charlie coughed and took the cigar out of his mouth. "I suppose, if you can call Barefoot Bubbly that."

David unwound the wire holding the cork. It didn't pop. He twisted it out, then grabbed off a shelf two large pig-shaped mugs with human faces, tongues protruding. They were crude but still his favorite ceramic pieces, the first he'd made when he'd taken up pottery, then sculpture, five years earlier at the age of fifty-four. He poured the pinkish wine into them and passed one to Charlie. David raised his mug and clinked Charlie's.

"To your return, and health. You look pretty good, Charlie. Thinner, but better than I expected."

Charlie took a long drink and rubbed his big beer belly. "Don't lie to me. Though better than *you* looked when you started working here." He stared at David's hairy chest. "A ghost, with an ugly zipper on its hairless sunken chest, but with a smile on its face that never quit. Like the ghost in that old comic book. What's its name?"

David smiled. Yes, a survivor once again, he thought, recalling the initial exhilarating feeling that somehow had persisted. "Homer the Happy Ghost."

After barely surviving the widow-maker, something had snapped inside of him when they stopped his heart and switched on the bypass machine. The previous David, the money-grubbing stockbroker, died. He now had a heart overflowing with joy, expressed spontaneously in whatever he created. He couldn't explain the miraculous burst of creativity, where it had come from or the form it had taken. But he'd stopped analyzing it and his transformation, afraid both might disappear as suddenly as they'd appeared.

David took a sip. "Delicious."

Charlie grinned. "You gotta be kidding. The heat in this shithole must be getting to you."

The sparkling wine was flat and too sweet, yet David loved it, just as he did anything new and different these days. Anything that didn't involve money. "How long's it been since you were here last? Six months?"

"Exactly a year next Monday, Labor Day."

"Sorry, I've been so distracted working on this I've lost track of time." Except for that time, the fifteen years wasted as a stockbroker, he still anguished over, wondering what had possessed him to leave academia and do that soul-devouring work. Then the enigma that still mystified him: how damn good he'd been at it, not that he was now proud of being his international firm's top producer, the Stockbroker to the Stars, as he was once called in a *Fortune* magazine feature article. He grew to hate the work, and himself. It wasn't him, he knew all along, his heart never really in it. Yet he kept at it, pushing himself harder and harder. Until his heart finally burst at the age of forty-nine. The best thing that ever happened to him.

Charlie laughed. "Distracted? From the looks of this . . . this monster . . . *obsessed* is more like it."

"I guess so. Had I started it then?"

"Just the head. Reminded me then of a zombie, the empty eyes. Now, with the supersized body, Frankenstein. Or Frankie's even uglier cousin."

David shrugged. "Take your pick."

"Why's the head so small compared to the rest of him?"

"It's my idea of a golem. Some say the inspiration for Frankenstein's monster in Shelley's book. And that disproportionately small head was the simplest way I thought I could show its main weakness, or perhaps the ironic contradiction the golem signifies."

Charlie licked his cracked lips. "Ironic contradiction? What the fuck are you talking about?"

"Golems are physically powerful and ostensibly invincible, but not exactly smart. Yet, that combination makes them the ideal helpers. They also can't speak, can't talk back. Perfect then for taking orders and, with their strength, for executing them successfully."

"Gollum? Like the weird character in that kid's movie?"

"*Lord of the Rings*, you're probably thinking. No, nothing like him, and this one's spelled g-o-l-e-m. The golem's a mythical human-like creature in Jewish folklore, and a mystical concept in the Kabbalah. The word's Hebrew, first used in the Old Testament. Psalms."

Charlie bent over and stuck his head right in front of the swamp cooler. "Never heard of that creature, but not surprising. Always skipped Sunday school."

"Wouldn't have mattered, it's not something that's taught there or even in Hebrew school. The word means an 'amorphous unformed mass' in Ancient Hebrew, a metaphysical construct that—"

"How 'bout in plain English for my chemo brain."

"An embryo, you could say. Talmudic scholars through the centuries have interpreted it in different ways as an abstract symbol. Some suggest it represents the malleability or variability of humans. Our potential to be compassionate beings, as well as to devolve into pure animals, shaped by our many innate shortcomings. Hate, greed, lust, to name but a few."

Charlie straightened up. "You're losing me again, professor, except for the lust part."

"We can't help ourselves. Intellectualizing, overanalyzing everything. Debating is a Jewish sacrament."

"Huh?"

"A statement almost as tautological as our propensity to—" David stopped, finally hearing himself, his old professorial voice, a relic from his first career as an anthropologist. "Forget that, you'll like this better. Golems, some believe, were *real* too, created by kabbalists—Jewish mystics—in medieval times to protect the Jews against persecution."

Charlie downed the rest of his wine and poured himself another cup. "Because they have superhuman powers? Like Frankie?"

"More like the Superman character, who not surprisingly was invented by two Jews. The way he uses them, intervenes to save people. Though golems are not nearly as good-looking as Clark Kent."

"That's for sure." Charlie stroked what was left of his once long and thick beard. "But if you ask me, they didn't do a good job protecting *your* people."

David nodded and looked past Charlie, at the wall behind him. Thumbtacked to a wood post leaning against it was a small, faded photo from 1938 of his mother, Sylvia, and her parents and siblings picnicking in Westpark in Munich. The last one ever taken of any of them.

David emptied his cup. "Unfortunately, golems were never really superheroes, their makers discovered. They were flawed, their power illusory, no different than humans. Unpredictable, too, like us. Difficult to control. Liable to turn on their creators, and those they were designed to protect, without warning or any reason. Playing God can be dangerous."

Charlie removed his hat and wiped the sweat off his bald head. "Are you saying those Jewish guys in olden days actually knew how to bring them to life? Magic?"

"In a sense. They animated them doing what Jews have always done best. Using their imagination, their chutzpah, and the power of words and numbers. Not to say a few tricks of the trade."

"Such as?"

"Esoteric incantations and arcane formulae, secrets passed down through the centuries we're not allowed to divulge." David smiled. "But I'll give you a clue. The same kinds of tricks we've mastered to control the world. You know, owning Wall Street, Madison Avenue, Vegas, Hollywood, the media, and all the money of course."

"Very funny. But something tells me, that glint in your eye, you know those secrets."

David winked. "Perhaps."

Charlies threw his hands up in the air. "C'mon, David, I'm your best friend. Show me how you do it, with Frankie here."

David peered at Charlie's large, rough hands that always reminded him of the selfless man, that genuine mensch he called Uncle Irving, a survivor also and his first best friend. The first person who truly understood him, and his pain. The father he never knew. A street peddler known as the Pretzel King of Brooklyn, and before that a Sonderkommando at Auschwitz, forced to shovel the bones and ashes of fellow prisoners, including those of his own family, out of the ovens. He never lost his sense of humor and faith in humanity. As a teenager, David worked alongside him, whose love of life was contagious. Now he could almost smell a freshly grilled pretzel as he pictured Uncle Irving showing him how to fan the charcoal fire with a piece of cardboard, at their hot pretzel stand on the corner of Bedford and Fulton in Brooklyn. And now he heard him say, *Do it gently, son. Like something you love.*

David blinked. "Maybe another time. But only if there's an urgent need. A bona fide life-or-death situation. According to those kabbalists, that's the only way it ever works."

"How 'bout then at your show's opening? Where there's sure to be an urgent need. Talk about life or death. *Death* mostly! I hate openings, they're so fucking boring."

"Me too. The posturing. The small talk. Even worse, the pretentious artspeak. A lethal combination that makes me want to shout *Stop* and head for the nearest exit."

"Please, old friend, do it there, if just for me. I could use a thrill. It could be my last."

The rumble of a freight train rattled the walls. David flinched and covered his ears, bracing himself for the whistle. The piercing blast shook him, but not nearly as profoundly as what came next, what that sound always triggered, the dreaded memory, the horrific stench of burning flesh.

"You know it's coming," Charlie said. "Yet that fucking whistle still scares the bejesus out of you every time."

David took a deep breath and let it out slowly, the memory fading away. "Sorry. What were you saying?"

"Bringing Frankie to life, at the opening, I hope."

"Okay, I'll give it a shot, just for you. But from what I've seen already, I doubt those young gallery folks will go for it. They're unlikely to think it's cool enough."

"But isn't the owner Jewish? That should help."

"She's a bagel-and-lox Jew. Wouldn't know a golem from a piece of gefilte fish."

Thunder boomed in the distance, to the south. They both turned their heads. "Yeah, that's more like it," Charlie said.

"Maybe we'll get lucky today."

Charlie put his hand on David's shoulder and flexed one leg, then the other. "I've got an idea. Why don't you suggest they advertise it as *performance art*. That'll make all them hipsters happy. Along with the free wine, cheese and crackers, it's sure to bring in a crowd."

"I think I'll bring chopped liver, kishke and knishes instead. More appropriate for the occasion, though not for that artsy crowd. And those delicacies, by the way, were a golem's favorite treats, his reward for killing Cossacks who carried out pogroms in the shtetels of Eastern Europe."

"Glad to see you haven't lost your sense of humor, even if your golem here shows none of it. That's what bugs me about this sculpture. It's so fucking serious, so different than all your other pieces. And I'm not sure I like it nearly as much as these." Charlie swept his hand toward the walls lined with surreal human faces and fantastical anthropomorphic animals fashioned of stone, wood, clay and bronze.

Through the doorway, David saw lightning flash in the darkening sky, and dust swirl in the parking lot. "Why?"

Charlie rubbed his thighs. "Gotta get off my feet, legs feel like jelly." He slumped down on the concrete floor covered with globs of dried plaster and paint. Breathing heavily, he fanned himself with his straw sombrero. "Ah, that feels better. But one of these days I'm gonna buy you a fucking chair. You never sit down, sit still, do you?"

"Too many years, I suppose, sitting at a desk. Thinking too much . . . about the wrong things."

Charlie laughed. "Thinking too much isn't something I'm familiar with. But doing the wrong thing is. Anyway, I'm not saying your sculpture's bad. The workmanship, I mean. Don't let this go to your head, it's finer than anything you've done before."

"What are you saying then?"

"It's creepy as hell, turns my stomach as much as the chemo does. The others here make me feel real good, make me laugh. They're all so funny. At least to me."

"And to kids. The only ones who ever get them."

Charlie's eyes narrowed. "Are you saying I'm a child? If so, look at me, David. I'm *not* laughing at your golem. It'd give *The Thing* a run for its money."

"Sure, it's no Rodin's *The Kiss*. But now you're exaggerating."

"Maybe. But what's gotten into you? Suddenly so dark. Or is it religious? Should I worry? Will you soon be chanting Hare Krishna or joining a Zen monastery? Going on a vision quest?"

David pictured Roberto, his vision quest guide and first mentor, standing with him twenty-five years ago in the monsoon rain on Tiburón Island in the Sea of Cortez. The sagacious old Seri Indian shaman showed him how to lick Otác, the psychedelic Sonoran Desert toad, and explained why to do it, what became the focus of a chapter in his book on the shamanic uses of Indigenous hallucinogens. The groundbreaking cross-cultural study that had made him at twenty-nine a rising star of anthropology. A world he'd soon abandon abruptly. He still didn't know why exactly. Only that it wasn't him, either.

"Done that, been there already," David said. "So don't worry. What I haven't done is *sell* any of my sculptures yet. Not that I really care about the money or need an ego boost. Just making it has been good enough for me. Making it for myself." David closed his eyes. "And . . ."

"And *what?*" Charlie swatted a mosquito on his forehead. "Where the hell are these little fuckers coming from? Never saw any when I was growing up here. Maybe they come along with all the folks moving here lately, the snowbirds and the rest of the other pests."

David kneeled on the floor facing Charlie. "But I'd get a kick out of selling this particular one. If only to hear someone say something other than 'It's *interesting*, David.'"

"All you need's the right name, something that sounds mysterious."

David pushed off the floor into a squat. "That's it! A rich snowbird who wants to convince others he's hip just might buy it then, thinking the sculpture must be profound, and that I'm a visionary." He laughed.

Charlie stared at the golem's face. "More likely you'll have to *pay* someone to take it. A crapload of money. It's that scary." He glanced up at the punch clock. "And the truth is that clock's the only part of it I understand. Sort of, anyway. Looks just like the one I punched for twelve years."

"At the Copper Queen Mine in Bisbee, you once told me about?"

"Right, working underground and nearly killing myself. But what's the clock doing up there? Makes about as much sense as mosquitos in the desert."

"Can't argue with that. Though some people will surely want to think it does, has some deep meaning."

"If it don't, why put it in there?"

"To me it's simply a joke. Like that silly sculpture called *Fountain* that was nothing more than a urinal on a pedestal. But the real joke is that art historians now claim it's one of the greatest sculptures of the twentieth century. Maybe if we also had a clever name for this one, it'd become famous too."

"Call it *The Time Golem*. Whatever the fuck that means, they're sure to eat it up. Then, finally, I'll be able to laugh whenever I see it."

David massaged his temples. "The *Time* Golem? Yes, that's enigmatic as hell. You're a genius, Charlie."

"Right—and Mother Mary was a virgin."

Mother, David said to himself. He glanced again at the photo of Sylvia and her—*his*—family, who, unlike him, hadn't survived. Weakened by starvation at Dachau, she died in the summer of '46 during the tuberculosis outbreak at Föhrenwald, the displaced persons camp. The following year, a Jewish aid organization placed David in a home for Holocaust orphans, on Decatur Street in Brooklyn.

David knew that if he'd put that picture in the shrine instead, the sculpture wouldn't be a joke. He saw his mother lying next to him at the camp, and felt her tremble beneath the rough wool blanket, heard her moan night after night, and knew why he hadn't.

"Listen," Charlie said. David refocused his gaze and shook his head. Charlie was staring at the metal roof. It sang with the patter of raindrops. David jumped to his feet.

"Shit, yeah! Give me a hand," Charlie said, extending his hand. David grasped it and, grunting, pulled him up.

David pounded his chest. "Don't you just love that sound? I've been waiting all summer to hear it again."

Charlie yanked down his overalls and ripped off his undershirt. "It's about fucking time. Bring it on."

Thunder cracked above them. Rain pummeled the roof. Wind whipped through cracks in the studio's walls. They ran outside. They raised their arms above their heads, pumped their fists, and together shouted "Yes!"

§

David was right: getting The Time Golem into the gallery was a bitch. The gallery was called End of the Earth, and the building's bones and setting fit the name. It was located on a once-blighted block of derelict gas stations, used tire shops, and taco stands. Built in 1928, it served first as the warehouse for a discount swamp cooler business that went bust soon after the 1929 stock market crash, and more recently as a home to a rat-infested recycled mattress factory that was soon condemned by the health department. Now it was the hippest art venue in town, thanks to the developer and owner, Emily Schwartz, the only child of an NYC power couple: her mother a corporate attorney for Ex-Lax by day and a stand-up comedian by night, who once opened for Jerry Seinfeld at Comic Strip Live; her father a self-made billionaire, the feared corporate raider nicknamed Sneaky Schwartzy, whose firm, Gideon & Company, was lauded far and wide for its generosity as a founder of the Museum of Jewish Heritage.

They'd removed the massive handcrafted mesquite wood entry door and disassembled the framing and elaborate ornamental metal grillwork. Four men tilted the sculpture sideways to clear the overhead beam. David watched as The Time Golem teetered precariously over the edge of the dolly.

Finally, directed by the exhibit designer, Lucia, they positioned it in the center of the gallery's "rustic" distressed wood floor, made of repurposed roughhewn barn boards. The worker Alberto went out to Charlie's battered old Ford F-100 pickup truck and grabbed the punch clock. He put it on the floor next to the sculpture. David and Charlie carefully removed the canvas sheet covering The Time Golem. Hector, the tallest of the workers, lifted the punch clock but couldn't reach up high enough to get it in the shrine.

"For god's sake, get a damn ladder," Lucia said.

"Don't bother," Charlie said. He took the punch clock from Hector and raised it above his head with ease and placed it in the shrine.

Hector turned to Charlie with his hand up for a high-five. "Gracias," Charlie said, slapping his hand. "I'll buy all you guys a Corona later."

The petite Emily entered the gallery from her glass-paneled office in the rear. She wore a silk Yves Saint Laurent tank top and sari skirt over black Prada combat boots. "Turn on the spotlights," she said to no one in particular as she approached the group. Lucia turned them on, then left the gallery, as did the workers.

Yes, Emily was a blueblood JAP with a reported nine-figure trust fund. Yet, in ways both overt and subtle, she belied the stereotype. Like her mother, she was as brainy, quirky and complex as they come, with a PhD in art history from Yale and a "master's" in the history of full moon worship from the Canarsie College of Wicca. Like her father, she was fearless in her work, but unlike him, her passion for risk taking was never motivated by money. At twenty-nine she'd already built a reputation as the peerless champion of the unknown outsider artist, the stranger the better, and had made her mark in NYC's highly competitive art gallery scene. Not surprisingly, some said Emily was only slumming it in Tucson—hardly an art mecca—and would soon be gone, back to her trendsetting, if controversial, Chelsea Black Hole Gallery, a name that others, her many enemies, said fit the art displayed there, not to say her soul.

Love her or hate her, no one could deny that Emily was a macher, or that her Tucson gallery had created the buzz responsible for transforming the seedy block and spawning the gentrification of Barrio Santa Rosa, the surrounding Hispanic working-class neighborhood. Cafés serving green smoothies, bookstore bars, vegan clothing stores, and the like were popping up left and right, and the nearby old adobe homes were being grabbed up and renovated by young hipsters arriving in droves from San Francisco and LA.

Emily stared at The Time Golem, her eyes and mouth open wide. "Oh my God, I had no idea. It's awesome."

"That it is," David said. "At least in the biblical sense of the word."

"A true original. You are a visionary, David."

"Hardly," David said, sweeping some strands of hair off his forehead. Hair he'd let grow long again. Almost as long as it had been in the sixties, though much straighter now in the desert, no longer the wild Jewfro of those days.

Emily twirled a long braid that extended down from

her magenta and electric-blue spiked hair. "You're much too modest per usual. It's monumental and revolutionary . . . literally, aesthetically, and spiritually. You are an outsider artist extraordinaire."

"I'd take outsider *literally*, and leave it at that."

"Don't be silly. Not only is your sculpture a master-piece, it's so timely and culturally relevant. Created and exhibited first in this city, a sanctuary for desperate refugees from south of the border. Just as New York once was for the Jews fleeing persecution. That's why I simply adore your idea of performing that ancient Jewish ritual at the opening."

"I'm glad you like the idea. I just hope the golem does too, and behaves. Doesn't run amok like the one in Prague did long ago and kill folks it was supposed to protect."

"I saw that old German silent movie *The Golem*, that I think you're referring to. It's based on a tall tale of course."

"Maybe not so tall a tale, Emily."

Emily laughed. "You're pulling my leg, of course. By the way, we'll be having a wonderful Klezmer band per-form at the opening. The group's all the rage now in Williamsburg. *Golem* is their name. Can you believe it? Amazing. A good omen, don't you think?"

"Amazing, I agree. But a good omen, I'm not so sure."

Emily leaned over the sculpture and patted the top of the golem's head. "And I just *love* the name you've given it. Genius. I have a client who'll drool over The Time Golem when she sees it."

Charlie grinned. "I almost shit my pants when I first saw it."

Emily straightened up and glared at Charlie. "Well, you're not exactly our target art collector, and please don't smoke in here."

Charlie tossed his cigar stub on the floor and walked away, muttering, "Thank God, you phony rich bitch."

Emily delicately squashed the stub with the toe of her combat boot. "What's gotten into your friend?"

David shrugged, though he knew exactly what had gotten into him. It was simple, nothing new. They came from completely different worlds and Charlie just hated Emily's privileged one, and her dictatorial style—*Imelda Jr.*, he'd begun to call her. David's own feelings about her were mixed, as conflicted as those behind his decision to accept her invitation to do the one-man show. If never really part of her world, he understood it intimately, had worked in it, and profited from it handsomely, kissing celebrity asses his daily penitence for taking their money. While her snobbery and pretentiousness also rubbed him the wrong way, he admired her ambition and passion—saw in her a part of himself his rebirth hadn't extinguished—and he did appreciate her unbridled enthusiasm for his work.

Emily glanced at Charlie, standing now on the other side of the gallery, in front of the water fountain. "Maybe he's still upset I didn't hire him."

A couple of years ago she'd asked Charlie to help with the renovation of the old mattress factory and its repurposing as a gallery. She'd wanted Charlie to do the decorative metalwork and had insisted on the same faux industrial chic design used at her Chelsea gallery. He'd refused, telling her, "I'm not about to replace the real thing with that phony crap."

David smiled. "Are you sure it wasn't the other way around?"

Emily fidgeted with the spaghetti straps of her skin-tight tank top. "Anyway, all we need is an equally brilliant artist's statement for Time Golem."

"I don't do those statements. Prefer to let my pieces speak for themselves."

"But, David, it's *conceptual* and philosophically complex, so it must be explained to heighten the viewer's experience. I may understand your piece, since I'm a student of Kabbalah. But the full meaning of it will be lost on most visitors unless—"

"A Kabbalah student, you say? I'm impressed. No wonder you grasp its full meaning. I'm not sure I do. You'll have to explain it to me then."

"Well, admittedly I'm a novice, have just begun studying at the Kabbalah Centre in New York, with the remarkable Rabbi Berg. His spiritual powers and ESP are legendary. Have you heard of his great teachings?"

David shook his head. "Only of his great success attracting celebrities, and what I read about his custom Bentley convertible."

Emily raised her left arm. It was covered with tattoos. "But I'm sure you recognize this." On her wrist was a red yarn bracelet. "Madonna, a fellow Kabbalah student and a close friend, gave it to me. She's also one of our best clients, and the one I mentioned that I think will be interested in buying Time Golem."

"I hope then you invited her to the opening. Now that she's Jewish, maybe she'll dance the horah and sing 'Hava Nagila' for us."

"I did invite her, but doubt she'll make it. She's in Europe, her Drowned World Tour. I'll send her some photos of it, though."

David pulled on the ends of his clipped graying mustache, even though there was little to pull anymore. Lately he'd considered letting it grow out too, into the walrus mustache of his hippie days.

"Do that, please," he said. "And give her the price. A million six, and a gross of those charming Kabbalah bracelets."

"That sounds fair, shouldn't be a problem for her. But back to the artist's statement. If The Time Golem is to be the centerpiece of this show, I insist you provide one."

"Sorry, not my shtick."

Emily fingered her gold and turquoise pendant—a leaping snow leopard, the endangered species that she told everyone was her spirit animal. "Well, then, I'll have to write it myself."

"Be my guest."

Charlie, still at the water fountain, coughed loudly, violently. David dashed over to him and put his arm around his shoulder. "Are you okay?"

"I'm fine," Charlie whispered. "Just needed your attention to hear me out. *Don't* let her do it. I don't trust the phony. Have your buddy Marty write it for you, she'll never know. And he'll be perfect, an expert at that sort of horseshit."

"My *buddy* is not exactly what I'd call Marty anymore. But you're right, intellectual gibberish is his specialty. So, as much as I dread listening to him pontificate, it wouldn't hurt to ask him to do it. And, if he agrees, it'll be fun to watch his ridiculous statement make her drool."

"Better yet, knock her designer combat boots off."

David walked slowly back to Emily. "I've changed my mind. I *will* write it. But on one condition. No matter what I write, you can't edit it."

§

On the curb outside of the entry to End of the Earth, David sat with his head in his hands. His old deerskin jacket kept his torso warm in the crisp November night, but his fingers felt stiff from the chill. He scrupulously kept his gaze cast down on the circle of light directly in front of him and tried to shut out the sounds of car doors slamming and heels clip-clopping on concrete as people arrived and entered the gallery. But he couldn't ignore the owner of the freshly polished Roper boots that shuffled into his line of vision.

"Buck up." Charlie leaned against the vintage Poul Henningsen lamppost that Emily had installed. "It'll be over soon."

The exaggerated voices of people attempting to hear one another over a frenzied punk rock rendition of "Shalom Aleichem" spilled out into the street. The night had a desperately festive feel to it. But it was Shabbat, after all, and everyone was eager to party again, 9/11 still fresh in their minds.

David kicked a broken G. I. Joe toy. "Not soon enough."

Charlie clamped his cigar in his mouth and pulled a whiskey flask out of the back pocket of his new 501s. "Take a few shots of this, it'll help."

David stood and took a long drink. "Don't know why I let myself get pulled into this." He passed the flask back to Charlie. "You look good." His friend's beard had regained its luster and his massive barrel chest once again threatened to unsnap the mother-of-pearl buttons on his Wrangler cowboy shirt.

"My new duds?" Charlie turned in a slow circle. "Bought them just for tonight. Nothin' but the best for you, man."

David reached into the pocket of his jacket, a relic from the sixties, his time in Maine trying to live off the land and sea. The same jacket he wore a few years later on the

Hippie Trail, trekking from Turkey to Nepal. He was sure he still smelled the Purple Haze he'd been stoned on for weeks in Katmandu. The jacket was appropriate for this occasion, he thought, if not as fitting as the other beloved relic he now touched with his fingertips.

Charlie took a swig. "Just make the best of it. Like I tried to do in 'Nam."

"Don't know how you managed, those horror stories you told me."

"Weed, lots of it. Then beer, in Germany, when I was foolish enough to reenlist. Though not as dumb as Dubya, sending more of us now to die in another shithole."

"You mean *Dumbya*? You never mentioned Germany to me."

Charlie slugged back more whiskey. "Too embarrassed I suppose to admit it."

"Where exactly?"

"Heidelberg."

David shut his eyes and dropped his head. "Ever do any sightseeing in Bavaria? Nuremberg or Munich?"

"Went to Nuremberg once. Saw the famous castle there."

"Not the Palace of Justice?"

"You mean where they had the Nazi trials?"

David nodded, opening his eyes.

"Not my idea of R and R. Never made it to Munich either, too far away."

David raised his head, stared at the moon, and mumbled, "It's only a twenty-five-minute train ride from Munich to Dachau."

"What?" Charlie said, then sniffed the air. David got a whiff of a familiar woodsy-spicy scent. Not that he knew the perfume's name: BVLGARI BLV for Men. Nor that it was favored by certain female movie stars, such as Kim Bassinger and Sarah Michelle Gellar. "Imelda Jr.'s coming. I'm gonna take a walk, see you inside." He squeezed David's shoulder. "Keep smiling, Picasso."

"*There* you are," Emily said, approaching David. She wore a long white sleeveless gown and a short black leather biker jacket. A reproduction of the iconic ensemble—sans crossbow—worn by Gellar in *Buffy the Vampire Slayer.*

David studied her outfit, noting the Lucite purse she held in her hand instead of the weapon. The image of Lori, thirty years ago, flashed before his eyes, his first love wearing a faded yellow slicker and holding a rusty old clam rake in one hand, pulling him close with the other as she kissed him in a tidal pool in Frenchman Bay, the two of them sinking deep in the mud, grasping for love in the feathery glow of a flower moon.

"Here I am," David said. "Unfortunately," he muttered. "Nice costume, and that vintage Charles Kahn purse is a classy touch."

"Thank you."

"But aren't you missing something essential, Dr. Schwartz . . . Ms. Gellar?"

"*You* never miss anything, do you, Dr. Klein . . . Mr. Stockbroker to the Stars?" She raised her left eyebrow. "The Renaissance Man of a Thousand Faces. Yes, she's my favorite actress, and *Buffy*'s my favorite TV show. But weapons of any kind always frighten me."

"That's one thing we do have in common."

"There's more, we both know. And I don't just mean our genes, the shtetels, pogroms, golems, and all the rest. Which is why I thought, hoped, you'd like me a bit more."

"I'm trying, Emily. But you make it hard. Your snobbishness."

Emily shifted her purse from her left hand to her right. "As if *you* are easy to like. What about your sarcasm? It hurts."

"Please don't take that personally, don't mean it to hurt. An uncontrollable defense mechanism, I suppose. I know that sounds like a lame excuse, but—"

"My father says the same thing about his jabs. He's a lot like you, though his comments are meaner and he never apologizes."

"Our tribe's way of dealing with the baggage we carry. Centuries of tsoris we can't shake. It's inside of you too. Just comes out differently."

Emily's glistening hot pink plumped lips parted slightly as she reached to grab hold of David's thin left wrist, the tattooed *179,331* barely visible anymore. "Please come inside, David. Everyone's dying to meet you, including a very special guest I invited but wasn't sure would come. Holland Cotter! You just might show up in the *New York Times*. What a coup for us! And I sense that, like everyone else here, he absolutely loves The Time Golem."

David pulled his arm away. "How can you tell? Is he drooling too?"

"There you go again. I overheard him talking to your friend Dr. Wisemann. Marty, is it? What a brilliant, charming man. They were just discussing your awesome artist's statement and Marty was raving about it. He wants to read it to all of us in the gallery, before you perform the ancient rite. A great idea, don't you think?"

"More like a dangerous curse."

"You're joshing me again, David."

"If he does read it, may the golem close his ears. Kinahora."

"What's that?"

"What your remarkable Rabbi Berg should say every time he gets into his Bentley. A blessing to reverse a curse."

A cell phone chimed its catchy ringtone, the thirteen-note passage from *Gran Vals*. Emily removed a sleek red Nokia 3310 from her purse.

"I bet that's your rock star rabbi calling," David said. "With his legendary ESP, he must've intuited we were talking about him."

"It's *her*," Emily mouthed. She listened for a couple of minutes, then said, "I just knew you'd love it. We'll hold it for you. Bye, bye. See you next week in New York, and we'll make the arrangements to have it shipped to you."

Emily put her phone back in her purse and, smiling, stepped toward David. "You won't believe this, but Madonna's buying The Time Golem for *three* million! She shared the photos I took of it with four of her friends from the Kabbalah Centre—Winona Ryder, Demi Moore, Paris Hilton, and Ashton Kutcher. My plan worked. They loved it too, and a bidding war started. Congratulations, David, you're no longer an outsider artist."

David stroked his nascent walrus mustache. "That's what I was afraid of."

"I'd get used to it if I were you, and celebrate. You're about to be rich and famous."

David laughed, or tried to, but what came out was a high-pitched squeak.

As if on cue, the band broke into their manic take on "If I Were a Rich Man."

"Listen, another good omen," Emily said and strode back into the gallery.

David followed her in, mumbling over and over, "Kinahora. Kinahora. Kinahora."

§

David stood next to The Time Golem and scanned the gallery, searching for Marty. He hoped he could somehow avoid him. Someone tapped his shoulder from behind and David turned around.

"Ah, the prodigal son, the enfant terrible of anthropology triumphantly returns," Marty said and bowed, holding one hand on his yarmulke. "The original Indiana Jones, the MacArthur Genius, the Wandering Jew of Wall Street and Katmandu, the Disappearing Doctor of—"

David raised his brows. "Are you done, Dr. *Shvitzer*?"

The short, chubby Marty straightened his striped crimson and cream bowtie. They had been colleagues in the anthropology department at the University of Arizona, when David lived in Tucson the first time. A Distinguished Regents Professor and acclaimed authority on non-Western art, comparative mysticism, dead languages, and anything else you asked him about, Marty held endowed appointments in four departments, a school record: anthropology, art history, philosophy and Judaic studies. And few would argue he belonged in a fifth, composed solely of himself—the pompous unbearable asshole he'd become.

"Not quite," Marty said. "Because I must applaud the Mysterious Misfit of the Millennium who finally graces us with his exalted presence." Marty clapped. "So many vunderlekh lives lived, so much shpilkes presumably transcended. And now this . . . this *meshuggah* creation. I don't know what to say. Except mazel tov!"

"But *I* know what to say, Marty, what no one else here but an old friend would. Your fly is at half mast, there's a chunk of potato knish on your Hush Puppies, and the leather elbow patch on the left sleeve of your corduroy jacket is hanging loose. If I didn't know better, I'd say that's the same one you wore when we were roommates at Harvard."

Marty shook the potato knish off his shoe, pulled up the zipper of his tan wide-wale corduroy pants, then fussed with the leather patch. He glared at David through his thick glasses. "How would you know? If I recall, you dropped out at the end of the first semester of your freshman year. And that fetching hippie jacket you're wearing is no doubt the same one you wore in Maine, when you joined the other dropouts going *back to the land*, stalking the wild asparagus, pretending to be hunter-gatherers, and failing miserably."

David smiled. "Touché. Shall we start all over?"

"If you insist."

"Thanks again for writing this—I think." David nodded at the artist's statement resting on a marble stand next to The Time Golem. "You really outdid yourself this time, if that's possible."

"I agree. It is a remarkable achievement, especially given the unmatched challenge of explaining what you created."

David laughed. "Are you actually going to read *all* nine pages to us tonight? Including your mind-numbing three-page footnote on the etymology of the word *golem* in Ancient Hebrew and Biblical Aramaic?"

Marty smirked. "*Read* it? Are you serious? Have you forgotten my photographic recall?"

"You never let me forget it, Marty."

"Speaking of which, when you came to my office to make your request, I forgot to mention that your son visited me last semester. Zach wanted a letter of recommendation. What a fine young man. Did you know he's applying to grad schools in anthropology?"

David pulled on the ends of his mustache.

"Probably not, I gather. Or that whenever I mention you to him he always changes the subject for some reason, as does your ex-wife when I ask about you at faculty meetings. By the way, Susan, you'll be pleased to hear—or not—just got a Guggenheim to study shamanism and Native hallucinogens in the Americas. Sound familiar? She's finishing the supposedly seminal work you didn't, one could say. I never understood why you left us . . . or *them*, for that matter."

I can't either, particularly them, David thought. His biggest regret, what he'd lost that hurt the most in his endless quest to find himself. "Enough already," he said and turned and walked away.

He weaved rapidly through the crowd, heading for the men's room. He hoped no one would recognize him. Susan would of course. What if she and Zach were here? Unlikely. They probably still hated him. And for good reason. He'd abandoned them in the middle of the night when Zach was two years old. For what exactly? Fame and fortune, wild sex, a more exciting life? No, another life that was but the same old lie, only the trappings different. When he was reborn after the heart attack, and returned to Tucson from LA, he'd tried to reach out to them to reconcile, make some sort of peace. He couldn't blame them for refusing. He'd been an asshole, his search for self-realization nothing more than selfishness.

The crowd was so thick in front of the bathrooms that he had to stop. Out of the corner of his eye he spotted someone at the bar waving at him. A stunning, statuesque blonde in a bubble gum pink dress and a sparkling choker.

She stood out from the crowd—and clearly recognized him. She sauntered toward him, a dazzling smile lighting up her face. Lilith. She'd been his client in the nineties when she wasn't quite famous yet, before the Oscar, but already a prima donna. The last one of his celebrity clients he'd talked to before almost dying.

"Don't pretend you don't recognize me, David," she said, holding a plastic champagne flute gracefully in her hand. "I know I'm getting old, but—"

"I recognized you, Lilith. How couldn't I? You're as lovely as ever," David said and kissed the hand she offered, that ridiculous antiquated gesture he knew she nevertheless loved. But one of several flirtatious hooks that he, the former lady's man—or was it womanizer?—had used to reel in other female clients throughout those years, though Lilith had remained his carnal queen and sole true siren, the one who understood him the best, his most reliable source of refuge and comfort, for which he should've been more grateful, especially those times when he wanted to end the life he'd come to despise.

Lilith squeezed his hand and pulled him closer, whispering in her familiar husky voice, "And you're as gallant as ever." She kissed him on the cheek, her intoxicating scent bringing back the memory of his hedonistic life, which then triggered the memory of Lori's salty scent, when she had taken him into her strong arms, her lips brushing his cheek, and whispered in his ear, "Be true to yourself, the poet you were born to be."

Lilith continued to hold his hand. "I was greatly saddened when I heard about your heart attack. And not just worried about my portfolio, I hope you realize."

"I realize that, Lilith . . . money was never that important to you," he lied and pulled his hand away. He stifled the urge to laugh in her face. He had been more like her than he wished to admit. Materialistic connoisseurs, consumed with the finer things in life—and with themselves. The only difference, perhaps, that she didn't seem to be aware of it. Lucky her, he thought, spared the consequences, the plague, of too much self-awareness. He was content with his new life, but he still sometimes woke up in the middle of the night tormented that he'd never shared much at all with anyone else, never loved anyone as much as himself.

Lilith slipped her foot out of her diamond-studded stiletto heels. "But I was thrilled to hear the open heart surgery was successful and you'd completely recovered."

"Yes, I was lucky. Lucky, too, my heart opened up."

"And, to be honest, I was also happy to learn you'd left the rat race. I'm thinking of doing the same. Reinventing myself, as you've clearly done."

"Clear maybe to you, but not always to me."

Lilith wiggled her bare toes. "I also want to do something more meaningful, spiritually satisfying. Focus on what matters most in life. After the Twin Towers attack, and now this insane War on Terror, my movies seem absurd. Especially the one that just came out."

"Haven't seen it yet. *Shallow* something or other, I think." David stared at her shapely foot and high heels. Standing in them, she was half a foot taller than him. Just like Lori had been, that summer of love, digging clams alongside him in her muddy rubber boots, or running barefoot with him through the swaying purple fields of wild lupine. Only, that's where the similarity to Lilith ended. He again pictured the sweet and innocent but tough and wise daughter of a poor clam digger. He saw and heard her quoting Emily Dickinson as she gave him the striped periwinkle shell she'd cherished. How had he managed to go from Lori to Lilith?

Lilith nodded. "That movie's so trivial now, I'm embarrassed. Humiliated."

"It's only the shock of the attack, reinforced by seeing the Towers collapse over and over on TV, that makes you feel like that. With time, you'll be yourself again."

Lilith's lush fuchsia lips—the same color as her toenails—pulled back into the sultry half-smile he also remembered well. "You always knew how to make me feel better."

An obese man, with long dirty hair and stinking of liquor, stumbled by them. He bumped into Lilith's shoulder, knocking the flute out of her hand, and walked away without apologizing.

"Yuck, let's get the hell out of here . . . go over there," she said, pointing to the gallery annex where his small sculptures were displayed, some of his earliest pieces. She slipped her foot back into her shoe and grabbed a bottle of champagne and another flute off the bar top. "It'll be quieter, David, more private to . . . reacquaint ourselves. I noticed that hardly anyone ever goes in there, or stays long. Don't know why."

I know why, David thought, and followed her in. Very few people liked those pieces, his satirical Crucifiction series, including *The Cellphone, The Laptop, The Hipster, The Foodie*. Though some got a kick out of *The All-American God*.

"This is much better," Lilith said when they were inside the dimly lit room. She poured champagne into her flute, took a sip, then offered it to David. "Try some. You used to love champagne. Remember that wonderful, rare bottle of it we shared to celebrate your first million-dollar day?"

David looked past her at *The All-American God,* a caricature in clay of Donald Trump, his face on the body of a hog, standing upright atop a model of Trump Tower. In one hoof he held a gold golf ball. In the other, a bottle of Dom Pérignon.

"Dom Pérignon, the 1996 Gold Edition," David said, his gaze still on the sculpture, his voice cracking.

"You seem distracted, nervous. But understandable. Stage fright, I'm sure. A form of performance anxiety, something I know a thing or two about. Go ahead, drink some. It always helps me on the set. It's La Grande Dame. Emily, like you, has such exquisite taste."

David shook his head. "Need to be clear headed for my . . . performance . . . later."

Not that it mattered. He might as well be drunk, still not sure what he'd do, except go through the motions, provide enough hocus pocus to give them what they came for and keep the mystery alive a while longer. Bring the golem to life? As big a joke as the punch clock?

Lilith stared at her champagne flute. "I like to think it helps me forget them for a while, but rarely ever does."

"Who? The people in the Towers?"

Lilith frowned. "No, those poor Muslims of course. Why do they hate us so, I keep asking myself. And not just us Jews. Maybe in my new life I'll help them, and others less fortunate than us."

"What do you have in mind?" He asked, though sensing what was coming.

Lilith closed her eyes. "I'm thinking I could give them practical tips on how to improve their lives, their health and well-being, build their self-esteem. The least I could do, for the women especially, my forté obviously. You are what you eat, as they say. Even what you look like. I'll show them what works for me. The benefits of natural foods and cosmetics, liquid cleanses, fasting, hot stone massages, Ashtanga yoga and Pilates."

"When you're worrying about where your next meal's coming from, I doubt hot stone massages will be high on the list of things you want or need."

Lilith emptied her champagne flute in one gulp. "But having a healthier lifestyle certainly can't hurt. What I'm now trying to do for myself, as well as simplify my life."

"I can tell by what you're drinking. And what you're wearing. Your Ralph Lauren Oscar gown and the Harry Winston diamond choker."

"Emily wanted me to wear something simple, soft, and romantic in pink, and something glitzy to go with her edgy outfit. Both iconic."

"*Elitist* is more like it, and one reason they hate us so."

"More of a joke, really, since both are copies. I had Ralph make me a shorter, simpler version of the original frilly floor-length gown. It would've been ruined on this splintery old wood floor. Or in the bathroom here, with those disgusting cockroaches, the biggest I've ever seen. I almost stepped on one. Ugh."

"God forbid."

Lilith lifted her foot and pointed her shoe at him. "And in *these* no less."

David lifted his foot and stomped the floor with his beloved old Frye boots. "The bigger the roach, the easier to squash, as we used to say in Do or Die."

"Do or die?"

"Bed-Stuy. Brooklyn, where I grew up."

"You never told me that."

"I never told you many things, Lilith. Did you know

that the ones in the Bronx are even bigger, nastier and smell worse? If you don't believe me, just ask Ralph Lauren, née Ralphie Lifshitz, that good ole Jewish boy from the Bronx, though now he probably won't admit it."

She touched her choker. "And these are fake of course. Wasn't about to wear the real jewels in this neighborhood."

"If you really want those poor Muslims to listen to you, rather than kill you when you show them what works for you, I suggest you wear a burka . . . and not one designed by Ralphie."

Lilith laughed. "I've missed your sardonic wit, Davy. Though not nearly as much as making love with you, and of course your specialty, the elegant way you'd first undress me. Slowly, smoothly, and always so creatively. I could tell how much you loved to do that, especially the erotic grand finale . . . removing my shoes. Like the ones I'm wearing. Stuart Weitzman's Cinderella Slippers, and not fakes. Elitist or not, I wore them tonight just for you. I'm surprised you haven't said a word about them, since they were your favorite. Don't you recognize them?"

David stroked his mustache. "Hard to believe you're really leaving show biz. It's in your blood. Hollywood royalty."

Lilith put one hand on a slender hip. "Actually, I'm from a long line of rabbis, in Poland. Religious royalty. Kabbalah masters, my father once told me."

"I never would've guessed."

"And I never would've guessed there was an artist inside of you, except in the boudoir. We're both full of surprises, aren't we? I love your sculpture, by the way. I really do. It's quite interesting. I considered buying it, and would . . . if I had the room now. But I've downsized, the first step in my plan to simplify my life. Who needs four homes anyway."

"Or four dozen different types of perfume. Some for the morning, others for the afternoon, and the best for the evening . . . when you're at your best."

Lilith stroked David's cheek. "You *do* remember me. Fondly, I hope."

David noticed for the first time the red yarn bracelet on her left wrist. "I see you find the Kabbalah *interesting* too."

"Jewish mysticism intrigues me. My roots, what we share. In fact, just the other day I was at a party and talked to my godfather about doing a movie with him. A comedic thriller about kabbalists, dybbuks, and golems, along the lines of his *Raiders of the Lost Ark.*"

"Didn't you just say you're through with all that?"

"It would just be a small part. Anyway, I want to rediscover my roots, as you have obviously."

David gripped the collar of his jacket and pulled it away from his neck. He wanted to remove it, but that would show his sweat-soaked blue denim shirt. "I wouldn't go that far. Still searching for them, and more."

"I wanted to see you again of course, but it's also the reason I'm here."

The band stopped playing. He'd soon be in the spotlight. "The golem rite? You may be disappointed."

"I doubt it, you've always been so humble. But I have to say I was shocked when Emily told me about who the sculptor was. I couldn't believe it was the same person, the David I once knew."

"You're not the only one. I often still ask myself who I am, if I've really changed."

"Well, I wouldn't worry. Trust me, you've changed,

and it looks good on you, very good." Lilith smiled that suggestive little smile, running her long slender fingers through her hair. "I like the new David a lot. Even more than the old one, who if you recall, I adored."

"I remember, but that was a different time, and now I'm—"

"Oh, shit, they found me again . . . more autograph hounds!" Lilith said, and jerked her head to the side. David followed her gaze out the annex's arched doorway. Five young women in Doc Martens, dressed all in black—with purple hair, face piercings, and spiked leather chokers— marched toward them. She sighed. "I must've signed fifty programs already, thought I was done. Maybe I am. From the looks of these, they're *your* groupies. Goth's never been my shtick."

"Mine or not, I'm leaving"

"Leaving them to me? That's not fair."

David stepped back. "Sorry, can't handle it now."

Lilith grabbed his hand, then squeezed it. "I understand," she said softly, and slowly let go. "I'm having a little party after the opening, at the Arizona Inn where I'm staying. Casita 6. I hope you'll join me then." She threw him another of her looks.

§

In the men's room, David removed his jacket, then splashed his face with cold water. He looked into the mirror, disgusted with what he saw. The truth. A weak fool who, if perhaps not exactly flirting with her, had certainly encouraged her seductive behavior. Kissing her hand, mentioning her perfumes and all the rest had the old beast rearing its ugly head. The sybaritic narcissist in him that hadn't really died on the operating table.

Casita 6, he mumbled to himself, shaking his head

from side to side. Lilith was hard to resist. But this wasn't anything new and different to embrace, something that would bring him joy. It was old, pathetic, and doomed.

He loosened his Lee Yazzie silver and turquoise bola tie, a gift from Dasan, the Navajo shaman who'd introduced him to the mysteries of peyote. A cockroach crawled out of the sink drain and onto the floor at his feet. Just as he was about to stomp on it, it flew off across the bathroom and smashed into a toilet stall.

He paced back and forth. He could use some peyote now. Why not? Maybe it would help him deal with the golem rite, at least make him forget who he was when performing it. Who knows, it might even allow him to disappear completely, shape-shift like Dasan had taught him and become the golem itself. Was that what those ancient kabbalists were actually up to? In an academic article he'd once written about shamanic shape-shifting in various cultures, he'd suggested that was likely the case.

While he'd never actually performed the rite, he'd researched it thoroughly, particularly the best-known version reportedly used by the revered kabbalist Rabbi Loew in sixteenth-century Prague. The one that had ended disastrously, with its distinctly Jewish, typically ironic, twist. Vivifying the golem? Pure folklore? Probably. The fantasy of a desperate people. Yet, his experience with highly accomplished shamans like Dasan and Roberto also told him that there was, indeed, another world out there, a magical realm that could be accessed. Still, he doubted he was the right person to do it. Neither was he made of the proper wizard material nor was his golem fashioned of the correct natural material needed to pull it off.

He walked out of the bathroom, scanned the gallery again, and spotted someone else who stood out from the crowd, only this one he was thrilled to see. He picked his way over to Charlie at the buffet table. He was stuffing three mini potato knishes into his mouth.

"I was afraid you wouldn't return," David said.

"Man . . . oh . . . man," Charlie garbled. He swallowed. "These are damn good. Maybe you should feed your golem some before you do your thing. Put him in a better mood."

"I doubt that'll work. They're not kosher. Nothing here is."

"You know I wouldn't miss your performance for anything, even having to listen to that windbag first. Looks like he's about to start, and you, old friend, look like shit."

"Thanks for reminding me. But thanks also for being here with me. This has been even tougher than I thought." He glanced at Marty, who stood next to the marble stand, Emily at his side. Marty picked up the artist's statement and flipped through the pages. Emily looked over the crowd with a broad grin across her face. She stepped forward.

"Hello Tucson!" Emily began. "Welcome to the art event of the year. Tonight the bright lights of the Old Pueblo shine deservedly on its very own visionary artist, David Klein, and his extraordinary creation, The Time Golem. David Klein's vision is cosmic, his sculpture timeless, as monumental as Michelangelo's *David* and as revolutionary as Duchamp's *Bicycle Wheel*. But far more meaningful than either to us today. In these unprecedented times of uncertainty and fear, of needless hate and suffering, The Time Golem gives us hope, opens our hearts to the truth, and answers the age-old question of why we are here on Earth. Yes, to love each other."

The crowd applauded loudly. Whistles and chants of "Guuulem! Guuulem! Guuulem!" broke out.

He had to hand it to Emily. She knew exactly how to

work a crowd. Seeing her in action, in her element, he realized he'd underestimated her. She was a Master of the Universe, like her father. But more, much more. Shrewd as they come. Radiant and supremely confident in the spotlight, with a powerful magnetic voice that shocked you at first, coming from such an insubstantial body. Then it hypnotized you. A force of nature you couldn't help but follow. Like Martin Luther King Jr. Or Hitler.

Emily strode into the crowd that surrounded The Time Golem. They parted as she approached and began to clap. She gestured with a hand to quiet them.

"We have a special treat for you tonight. We're honored to have with us Dr. Martin Wisemann, the renowned scholar, the world's expert on Jewish mysticism. Professor Wisemann, using David's awesome artist's statement and adding his own erudite commentary, will help us understand the meaning of The Time Golem and why it may be the most important piece of art you'll ever see. So please listen carefully to this enlightening entrée to David's performance of the ancient rite, one that promises to bring the golem to life and deliver its message of peace. What the world needs so desperately now. Yes, the time has come to give peace a chance. Shalom."

The golem's message of *peace,* David thought. A new twist on the golem tale, and clever as hell. Leave it to Emily to find exactly what the crowd wanted to hear. Inexplicably, he suddenly felt better. Much calmer. It must be Charlie, having his friend at his side. Or was it the charismatic Emily? He glanced at the enraptured faces in the crowd. Maybe, like them, he'd been entranced by her.

Charlie elbowed him in his ribs. "Can't wait to hear your buddy. This is gonna be good."

"Good, if you need a long nap."

Marty pushed his glasses up the bridge of his nose, then, as was his custom whenever he began a lecture, patted his yarmulke. "The Lord God formed a man from the dust of the desert," he said in his nasal monotone. "And He blew into his nostrils the breath of life, and the man became a human being. Genesis 2:7, one of the two creation stories in the Torah, the Five Books of Moses. which I'm sure you are all familiar with." Marty snickered. "Those few among us today who still read, that is. Well, if you do, and even think occasionally, then you must ask yourself if this is but a myth, no different than that of the Hopi's origin story whereby they, the first humans, emerged from beneath the earth's surface. Or what the kabbalists believe, that Adam was in fact a golem, the first, before that Divine Breath. And since God made him in his own image, Genesis 1:27, then God is a golem too, theologically speaking. Thus, a priori, we *all* are golems, epistemologically speaking or not. Indeed, an intriguing, sobering thought that I wish to leave you with tonight, if the least profound of those that I will offer about the meaning of—" Marty gestured theatrically at The Time Golem—"what we've all come here to see.

"When one views *The Time Golem* for the first time, the eye is drawn immediately not to the figure of the golem itself, the ghostly visage notwithstanding, but to the punch clock in its prominent position atop the sculpture, noting its incongruity, even its absurdity. In drawing our attention to it, the artist seems to be suggesting that the sculpture's meaning lies there. A shrine to modern man's obsession with and enslavement by time. Or, perhaps a shrine, however perverse, to that more fundamental human flaw, our common fate, our mortality, an immutable condition that not even the omnipotent golem can ever change."

Marty rambled on for several more minutes, giving a half dozen other progressively abstruse interpretations of the sculpture's meaning.

Charlie's eyes had closed, his head slumped to his chest. David kicked his foot. "Wake up."

Charlie lifted his head and shook it from side to side. "Why? Was I snoring?"

"You're missing the best part—not!"

"Shit, this dude's too much, a real downer. Sounds like a nerdy robot on ludes. Makes the talking computer in that old space movie sound human by comparison."

"True, and HAL had something going for him that Marty doesn't. A touch of humor, and not just any. After all, the movie's director was a New York Jew. I wouldn't be surprised if Kubrick had a golem in mind when he created HAL and had him wreak havoc on the crew."

"I thought you said golems can't talk."

"If they could, that's how they'd sound, with a Jewish sense of humor."

"Don't know about that. But do know that Marty obviously doesn't hear himself."

"Oh, he hears himself alright, loves the sound of his own voice. And 2001 is here much sooner than we thought."

He glanced over at Emily. She waved at Marty, then pointed her index finger in the air and moved her hand in a small circle. The universal sign to wrap it up. David turned to look at the throng. Someone covered a yawn, and the murmur of conversations grew louder. A couple headed for the door. He looked back at Emily and saw her whisper something to one of the band members.

Marty cleared his throat and began to speak much louder. "I will offer one final, truly original exegesis of The

Time Golem's meaning. One far more apropos of our doomed world, if suggested and prophesized by what happened four centuries ago in Prague, when the first artificial man, the golem created by Rabbi Loew, acted in a seemingly bizarre fashion, as noted earlier. I suggest that the golem, as represented in this sculpture, is a universal symbol of the dark side of knowledge, of advanced technology, our so-called progress in this sinking modern world. Indeed, of the dangers embodied in the development of the atomic bomb, genetic cloning, the computer, artificial intelligence generally and all the rest that is purely man-made, surpassing nature as the dominant force in human life. The silent spring, the fossil fuel inferno, the coming nuclear winter, our own Tower of Babel collapsing, Joshua's trumpet blasting—yet we remain glued to our TVs, watching *The Simpsons*. The implications are foreboding for the future of mankind, and so I need to elaborate. But first it is essential that you understand the etymology of the word 'golem' in Ancient Hebrew and Biblical Aramaic and, hence, its original meaning, which will shed light on the subsequent translations in Greek and Roman that distorted it. And finally, the pièce de résistance, my admittedly unique reconstruction of how the Kabbalah restored the truth. So, let me elucidate."

Marty droned on for another ten minutes, then Emily signaled the band to start playing.

She trotted up to Marty and shook his hand. "Thank you, Professor Wisemann. That was truly . . . special." She pivoted back to the crowd. "And now for the performance we've all been waiting for. The mystical golem rite. The first time it's been performed in over four hundred years. Prepare yourself for a uniquely enlightening experience of peace."

The gallery lights dimmed, except for the spotlight on The Time Golem. The audience quieted and the drummer tapped a drum roll. David took a step forward and froze in midstep. "I can't do it," he whispered.

Charlie put his arm around his shoulder. "What the hell happened to the David I know? This should be exciting for you. Remember how happy you were when you first played with clay in your studio? I do. That shit-eating grin on your ugly face. This is no different. It could even be more thrilling than anything you've done before in your life. A ride into the unknown."

"I hear you, but—"

"No buts, go for it. Stop being a wuss. C'mon, what do you got to lose anyway? You . . . both of us . . . could be dead tomorrow."

David took a deep breath, then another, and it hit him—he was still breathing. He felt the scar itch on his sweaty chest, his heart still beating, then pictured that first time he held clay in his hands. The exhilaration as he began to mold it, not knowing what form it would take. He smiled, if weakly, feeling at least a trace of that familiar wave of joy rush through him. "What the fuck, I'll do it. Do it my way."

He walked rapidly to his sculpture. He bent over the golem's head and breathed into its nostrils and whispered, "I'm not God, and you're not Adam, not even close. So, we'll roll the dice and let them fall where they may."

He pulled out of his jacket pocket another relic from his days in Maine. An awl he'd made himself. The awl he and Lori had used to engrave their names into the gnarly trunk of the stunted scrub pine under which they'd sat and talked and made love all summer long. He could see her that glorious day at the end of the summer when she used the awl to engrave a heart around their names.

He took the awl and engraved *EMET*, the Hebrew word for *truth*, on the golem's forehead. Just as Rabbi Loew had done. In other versions of the golem rite, one or another of the sacred names of God were inscribed, particularly the tetragrammaton, the holiest of the holy, the ineffable name written *YHWH*. He considered using it, but *truth* seemed most appropriate for him, and what he thought he'd then do, if still only a vague plan to be executed on the fly, the only way he knew how to create art.

David slowly circled the golem the ritually prescribed ten times. *Ten,* the kabbalist's power number representing the ten divine emanations of the Ein Sof—the Infinite. Instead of meditating on them to release the mystical energy needed to vivify the golem, as the Kabbalah dictated, he breathed in and out slowly and rhythmically while circling the golem, focusing solely on his breath, the form of meditation-in-action he knew best from his time long ago at the Zen monastery and farm where he'd worked in the kitchen and the fields. With each inhalation he intoned the last koan that the Zen master Alan had given to him, the question he'd never managed to answer—*Who am I?*

Circling the golem the tenth time he heard a faint rhythmic thumping, like the lub-dub sound of the heart heard through a stethoscope. He placed the palm of his hand over his heart. No, that wasn't the source, because he now felt the room itself, the air itself, pulsate in the same subtle rhythm.

Did others also feel it? He stopped walking, peered out into the gallery, and listened. It was absolutely silent and still, his vision, his mind, blank. The thumping was now gone—and so was he. He was that silence, that stillness, that nothingness. That wholeness? He turned toward his sculpture. Was he now the golem too?

Staring up at where the shrine would be, he did a double take. Not only could he see clearly now, but the punch clock had disappeared. In its place was a grilled pretzel, cut in half, its tantalizing aroma making him smile. He heard the thundering belly laugh of Uncle Irving, then his thick Yiddish-accented voice. *Time to be a mensch, and share your pretzel, son.* David's smile broadened.

The pretzel disappeared. He sat on the floor next to the golem's feet and resumed his meditative breathing. The scent of the sea, the mud, and Lori filled his nostrils. He opened his eyes. Lori's striped periwinkle shell, that he'd foolishly thrown away, now rested inside the shrine. *I brought it back to you,* she whispered. *To remind you of the love we shared. Of the beautiful poem you wrote and gave me. "Love in the Mud." And that it's time for you to love again.*

The shell disappeared. He heard loons moan and splash as they dove into the sea. Then the voice of the Zen master Alan. *You'll find it—who you are—when you stop seeking and start listening to the loons.*

He smelled a Gila monster roasting on a spit over a mesquite wood fire. The crude ironwood carving of the Sonoran Desert toad he'd made and given to Roberto, the Seri Indian shaman, appeared in the shrine. A gift for showing him the truth. *I have nothing to teach you Davy that you don't already know in your heart is true,* he heard Roberto say. *Let what's in it be your teacher.*

The carved toad disappeared. He smelled burning human flesh and saw Sylvia sleeping next to him at the death camp. She sat up suddenly and screamed, *Zol er krenken un kedenken!* He shuddered at the sound of the curse. He watched himself wrap his little arms around his mother's neck, snuggling and comforting her. He blinked, then saw himself staring at his tiny left wrist, the tattooed number gone.

He sat unmoving at the golem's feet, content to just sit and listen to his breath. He doubted he had the answer to the koan, but he could care less. He knew in his heart that now he had something far more precious.

Footsteps echoed around him. He stood, feeling light-headed, yet relaxed and focused. He looked out into the gallery. Except for the band packing up, it was empty.

From behind The Time Golem, Charlie appeared, beaming, a brown paper bag in his hand. He hugged David. "What you just did was *awesome*, as Emily would say."

"What do you got there? A souvenir?"

"This?" Charlie said and held up the bag. "Wasn't about to let them throw away any of those knishes. Got the munchies real bad after you finished. Just like in 'Nam after getting high."

"Not sure what I did, but know what I want to do now. Did you see or hear anything . . . unusual?"

"Only *felt* something unusual, though can't describe it easily." Charlie closed his eyes. "A weird kind of quiet. Like everything suddenly stopped. And then the craziest thing. It was as if I wasn't here anymore, but somehow part of it all. Does that make any sense?"

David nodded, smiling.

"Yeah, it was strange as hell, yet incredibly soothing. A calmness that swept over and filled me, like nothing I've known before. Maybe I'm imagining it, but from the looks on the faces of others in the gallery, their smiles just like yours now, they felt it too. Even Marty, which is saying something."

"I also felt it. Still do."

"I can tell, you look different. Not just happy, but peaceful. And I still feel it too, I think. Still am high anyway. Wanna share a knish, or two?"

"Kinahora," David said, then laughed. "Probably best not to talk about it anymore, or we'll jinx it."

"Just one more thing, then I promise to shut up. I've been wondering if Emily also had something to do with what just happened. And I don't just mean organizing the show. Maybe she's not as bad as I thought. I'm even beginning to think I like her. I know, hard to believe. But she seemed to have helped us to feel it, when she told us the golem would bring peace."

"Like the golem, we all have it in us to be a mensch. Can you give me a hand, lift me up to the shrine."

Charlie lifted him up. David removed the punch clock and clutched it to his chest as Charlie let him down slowly. David set it on the floor. "Now once more."

Charlie lifted him up again. David pulled the old photo of his family out of his jacket pocket and placed it inside the shrine.

About the Author

Seth Schindler is an anthropologist, sculptor, Zen archer and writer of fiction and nonfiction. He has worked as Curator of the Arizona State Museum, and served as NEH Fellow at the University of Arizona and Weatherhead Resident Scholar at the School for Advanced Research. His short stories have appeared in many literary magazines. His novelette *Licking the Sacred Toad* was a finalist for the Gival Press Short Story Award. The University of Arizona Press recently published Dr. Schindler's book about the plight of the food insecure in America today, *Sowing the Seeds of Change*.

Made in the USA
Middletown, DE
24 November 2024